ZOE Gets READY

By Bethanie Deeney Murguia

ARTHUR A. LEVINE BOOKS
An Imprint of Scholastic Inc.

Library of Congress Cataloging-in-Publication Data

Murguia, Bethanie Deeney.

Zoe gets ready / by Bethanie Deeney Murguia. — 1st ed.

p. cm.

Summary: Zoe wonders what kind of day she will have as she prepares to get dressed on Saturday—the only day of the week on which she can
decide for herself what to wear.

ISBN 978-0-545-34215-5 (hardcover : alk. paper) [1. Clothing and dress—Fiction.] I. Title.

PZ7.M944Zoe 2012

[E]—dc23

2011027694

Book design by Elizabeth B. Parisi

10 9 8 7 6 5 4 3   12 13 14 15 16

Printed in China 38 · First edition, May 2012

The artwork was created in pen-and-ink and watercolor.

In loving memory of my dad,
grandfather to the real Zoe and her sister

On school days, soccer days, and rainy days, someone else always chooses what Zoe will wear.

But today is Saturday,
and that means Zoe gets to decide.

"I know!" she says.
"I'll have a pocket day,
definitely a pocket day.

I'll collect more treasures than ever before."

"Almost ready, Mama.

Hmmm, then again..."

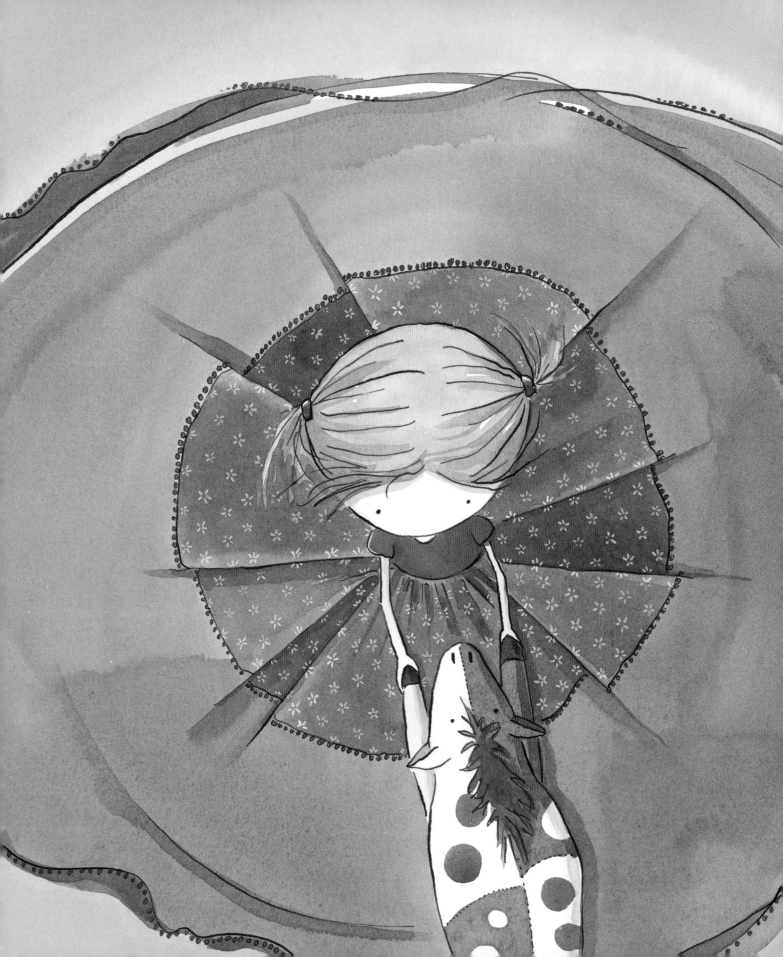

"I might have a twirling day, a dizzy, whirling day.
I'll spin and spin till I'm as light as a feather."

"On the other hand . . ."

"This could be a cartwheeling day —
a bouncy, feet-in-the-air day.

My toes will tickle the clouds."

"Just getting organized!"

"Maybe I'll have an exploring day.
I'll lead the way to secret places."

"Or a stand-out day?"

"How about a touch-the-sky day?"

Zoe stops.

And then she knows exactly what to do.

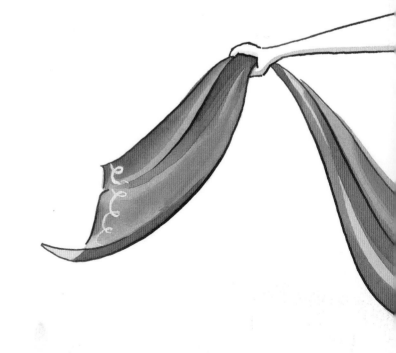

"Ready, Mama. And no mess!"

"Wait," remembers Zoe.
"Just one more thing."

And now Zoe is ready for her day.